MAGIC, MAGIC
EVERYWHERE

by Perdita Finn

Little, Brown and Company
New York ✳ Boston

Cover design by Véronique Lefèvre Sweet.
Cover illustration by Laura Thomas.

Little, Brown and Company
Hachette Book Group
1290 Avenue of the Americas, New York, NY 10104
Visit us at lb-kids.com
MLPEG.com

First Edition: June 2017

Little, Brown and Company is a division of Hachette Book Group, Inc. The Little, Brown name and logo are trademarks of Hachette Book Group, Inc.

The publisher is not responsible for websites (or their content) that are not owned by the publisher.

Library of Congress Control Number 2017935526

ISBNs: 978-0-316-43186-6 (paper-over-board), 978-0-316-43187-3 (ebook)

Printed in the United States of America

LSC-C

10 9 8 7 6 5 4 3 2 1

For my own magical friends...
Denise, Marijo, Bev, Lynn, Priscilla,
Susan, and Linda.

CONTENTS

✴ ✴ ✴

CHAPTER

1

Shimmers and Shivers

★ ★ ★

Sunset Shimmer was writing in her diary outside of Canterlot High. There was so much to tell Princess Twilight Sparkle. But her magical book was the only way to send word from the everyday world of Canterlot High to the enchanted realm of Equestria. Sunset

Shimmer sighed. She needed advice from her friend. She was worried.

Dear Princess, she wrote, *I can't seem to keep my mind on anything other than our new powers and the magic that exists in this world, and how scary but exhilarating it all is.*

Sunset Shimmer touched the sparkling geode that hung around her neck. It came from the crystal cave at Camp Everfree that the girls had discovered. Each of the girls wore their geodes now—and they seemed, somehow, to give the girls powers they'd never had before. Sunset Shimmer was convinced that magic was somehow seeping into the world from Equestria. But how? Why? What were they supposed to do with it?

How can we be prepared for it? she asked her friend. *When will it show up again? You see the problem. I can't seem to stop stressing when there's nothing going on. With the weight of all Equestria on your shoulders, you must have some advice on how to*

She turned the page to keep writing— but there were no more pages in her diary. She had used it all up! "Oh no, no, no, no!" She gasped.

"What's the matter, Sunset Shimmer?" It was Pinkie Pie. She and the other girls were carrying buckets and sponges over to the parking lot. They'd organized a car wash to raise some money to repair Camp Everfree. The girls had managed to save the camp from being sold—but now they had to find a way to pay for everything that needed to be fixed, and they were determined to do so. But it was going to be a lot of work.

"I ran out of pages in my journal, that's all," she fretted. She was on the verge of tears.

"Chillax, SunShim," said Rainbow Dash, patting her on the back.

"Who's SunShim?" Fluttershy asked.

"That's my new nickname for Sunset Shimmer. I just made it up!"

Twilight Sparkle frowned. She was particularly sensitive to how others were feeling, and noticed that her friend was more upset than she was letting on. "There's more bothering you than just journal pages, isn't there, Sunset Shimmer?"

Sunset Shimmer shrugged. She didn't want to worry the others.

"C'mon!" Pinkie Pie laughed, cheerful as always. "Share your troubles. It might help soothe your stressed nerves."

She looked at the girls, all ready for the big car wash. "I don't want to take any of the fun out of our big event...."

"I said spill it, SunShim!" Pinkie Pie ordered her with a giggle.

"Okay, okay." Sunset Shimmer smiled in response. "It's just that things have been calm around here, magic-wise."

"And that's a bad thing how, exactly?" Rarity was much happier to be designing fashions again than trying to save her friends from out-of-control vines, the way she had to at camp when the powerful Gaea Everfree possessed Gloriosa Daisy.

Sunset Shimmer looked up at the clear, blue sky. Students were milling about on the steps of Canterlot High after classes. Her friends looked upbeat and happy.

Still, her eyes fell on the crystal geodes that hung around each girl's neck. They'd found them in the crystal cave at Camp Everfree. The geodes gave all of the girls special magical powers—from being able to run superfast like Rainbow Dash to creating sparkling clouds of sprinkles like Pinkie Pie. But how had those geodes become enchanted? That was what worried Sunset Shimmer. Magic was seeping into their world from Equestria—and even if they could control their own newfound powers, what if magic fell into the hands of someone who couldn't?

"It's just that instead of enjoying the fact that everything is calm, I'm constantly thinking about what will happen when it won't be."

Fluttershy smiled nervously. "It won't?" she asked.

Sunset Shimmer sighed. "See? That's what I'm talking about. I shouldn't even be thinking about this stuff right now. And neither should any of you."

Pinkie Pie dropped her bucket, and water

splashed everywhere. Her eyes wide, she stared at the magic diary. "Look! Princess Twilight's writing you back!" A swirly scrawl of words was appearing on the diary's back cover. Pinkie Pie giggled. "Sunset's getting an Equestritext!"

"What's it say?" asked Applejack curiously.

Sunset Shimmer was stunned. This was not what she'd expected. At all. This was big news. "Princess Twilight wants me to come to Equestria," she told the others.

They stared at her. This was a surprise.

"But what about our car wash?" asked Pinkie Pie.

"I'm sure the princess will understand if I help you out first," Sunset Shimmer answered. "After all, that's what a good friend would do...."

But why would the princess need her in Equestria? Was something the matter after all?

CHAPTER

2

Splashes and Bubbles

★ ★ ★

Buckets of soapy water and hoses were all over the parking lot. A huge sign was draped over the back wall of the high school. The girls were cleaning up a beat-up, old truck.

"To the right! To the right! To the left! To the left!" chanted Pinkie Pie as the girls scrubbed with their brushes.

"Now up! Now up! Bring it down and around! Wash that car like you mean it!" Pinkie Pie twirled round and round, laughing with delight.

Rainbow Dash sped from one car to another, polishing and shining each and every one. Fluttershy and Rarity were vacuuming the insides of each car carefully. Applejack happily lugged bucket after bucket filled with soapy water over to the girls. Sunset Shimmer was making sure every passing car stopped for a cleaning, and Twilight gave every vehicle a gleam and sparkle that was especially hers.

The geodes around their necks glowed, but the girls weren't using their magic to help out. They'd had enough experiences with magic to know that they should use it carefully. It could get out of control so easily…and it had in the past.

The girls stepped back and admired their work. Rainbow Dash knocked on the window and Big Mac rolled it down. He handed Rainbow Dash a few dollars.

"Thanks!" said Rainbow Dash. She counted it out as the truck sped off. "Sweet! More cash to add to the stash!"

"Woo-hoo!" Pinkie Pie cheered and high-fived Rainbow Dash, who put the money in a pink lockbox. They'd had a really busy afternoon.

Rarity was tired. She wiped some suds off her forehead. "Yuck. How about a little break? All this sunshine and soap is doing a number on my hair." Rarity had thought about using her diamond dome to protect her outfit while she worked, but it just didn't seem like a good idea. Her diamond dome was only for emergencies. Anyway, weren't you supposed to get sudsy at a car wash? She grabbed some sodas from a cooler and began handing them out to the girls.

Rainbow took a long drink. "Hey, anybody seen Twilight lately?"

"I'm here!" Twilight was sitting on the curb. She was punching the buttons on a calculator, clearly frazzled. "I was just going over the numbers again."

"Have we raised enough to make all the repairs to Camp Everfree?" Sunset Shimmer asked.

Twilight adjusted her glasses. "We've only raised half. I counted the money four times just to be sure."

It was just like the sun had gone behind

the clouds. The girls frowned. They'd been working so hard.

"Hey, it's all right." Applejack always tried to look on the bright side of things. "We can just wash more cars. There's gotta be some we missed."

The girls scanned the empty parking lot. All the cars were gone. They'd all been washed.

"I think we're going to have to come up with a new plan," suggested Sunset Shimmer. Maybe the princess would have an idea when she went to visit her.

"But we're running out of time!" worried Rainbow Dash. "The money is due next week and Pinkie Pie's already hosted a bake sale. Twilight and Fluttershy had that doggie day care, and we've done this car wash."

"What else can we do to raise money?" Fluttershy wondered aloud.

"I wrote to the director of the Daring Do movies," Rainbow Dash admitted. "He went to Camp Everfree, and I thought he might help us. But I never heard from him."

Everyone looked glum.

"Not to worry, darlings," announced Rarity with determination. "It's my turn to devise a plan, and I already have something amazing in mind. It will be the most profitable of all our fund-raising events! The pièce de résistance!"

Applejack clapped her hands, excited. "Now we're talkin'! What's your idea?"

"Meet me in the music room later this afternoon and I'll explain everything." Rarity smiled mysteriously.

"That gives me time to talk to Princess Twilight, too!" said Sunset Shimmer.

"Exactly," Twilight Sparkle nodded in agreement.

The girls raced off to clean up. Thank goodness for Rarity! Now they would be sure to save Camp Everfree. But the only one who didn't look happy was Rarity herself. She stayed frozen in the parking lot after everyone was gone. She wasn't smiling anymore. She looked completely panicked.

Spike, Twilight Sparkle's talking dog, looked up at her. "You got nothin', huh?"

"How did you know?" Rarity was on the verge of tears. Everyone else had sponsored such good fund-raisers, and she wanted to do her part; she really did. But what could they possibly do to raise enough money to save Camp Everfree? She had no idea.

CHAPTER

3

glimmers and gleams

* * *

Sunset Shimmer approached the statue of the Wondercolt. It had been a long time since she had gone back to Equestria. Timidly, she touched the colt's hard hoof. Her hand went right through the stone. It disappeared.

Sunset Shimmer shut her eyes. She took

a big breath—and she jumped. It was like being on a roller coaster that went upside down and around and around, again and again. She twisted and turned; she flipped and flopped. A moment later she hurtled out of a mirror. She skidded across the shiny surface of a marble floor and careered into a bookshelf on the opposite wall. She was in Princess Twilight's library in the Castle of Friendship.

She shook herself off. Her ears and her tail twitched. She was a pony again, but she was too dizzy to stand up. She groaned.

The soft face of a friendly pony loomed over her. Sunset Shimmer blinked, trying to get her eyes to focus. "Princess Twilight? Is that you?" she asked.

"Nope!" came a voice. "Starlight Glimmer."

Sunset Shimmer staggered to her hooves. "Whoa," she whinnied. "That feels a little weird after all this time." She wasn't used to having four legs anymore.

She looked at the perky purple pony standing in front of her. "Starlight Glimmer," she remembered, "you're Twilight's student, right?"

"Uh-huh." Starlight Glimmer nodded. "She wanted me to give you this."

A journal floated through the air toward Sunset Shimmer.

"She wanted to give it to you herself," explained Starlight Glimmer.

"But I came too late!" realized Sunset Shimmer.

"No, no, no," Starlight Glimmer rushed to reassure her. "She understood you needed to help your friends with their fund-raiser, but she was called away to solve an urgent friendship problem of her own. That happens a lot around here."

Sunset Shimmer sighed. "So I'm probably not going to see her?"

Starlight Glimmer just shook her head apologetically. "Sorry. She just told me to give you the journal."

Sunset Shimmer held it with her hoof. It was a relief to know she could get in touch with the princess. Still, she had really hoped to see her. "So, um, I guess I'll be going now." She turned back to the mirror and prepared herself to enter the portal again.

She was lifting up her leg to leap when Starlight Glimmer stopped her. "What's it like back there?"

Sunset Shimmer whirled around happily.

On Starlight Glimmer's face was an expression of deep curiosity.

"It's pretty different," Sunset Shimmer told her. "And not so different at the same time. It's kind of hard to explain."

"Guess you kind of have to go there to really get it, huh?" Starlight Glimmer snuck a glance at the mirror. "I, uh, don't suppose..."

Sunset Shimmer realized that she was asking to go with her to visit Canterlot High! "You really think Princess Twilight would be okay with that?"

Starlight Glimmer shrugged. "I don't know for sure that she *wouldn't* be okay with it."

"That's not really a particularly compelling argument," Sunset Shimmer noted. She didn't want to get in trouble with the princess.

But Starlight Glimmer rushed to offer an explanation. "She wants me to learn as much as I can about friendship. And I'm not learning a whole lot just hanging out here in her castle."

Sunset Shimmer took in this information. It was true. There was no rule about ponies not visiting Canterlot High, after all. Also, she didn't think there would be any awkward run-ins with Starlight Glimmer's human counterpart. "I haven't seen you in that world," she said. "So chances are you aren't going to run into yourself—"

"That's not something you hear every day!" Starlight Glimmer interrupted, laughing.

What else could possibly go wrong? Sunset Shimmer was trying so hard to be responsible. Still, it would be nice to have someone from Equestria nearby. "Lay low," she told Starlight Glimmer. "Don't draw too much attention to yourself."

"You'll barely even notice I'm there!" Starlight Glimmer was clearly thrilled. She was going to Canterlot High. She knew it.

"Introducing you to my friends will be a nice distraction," admitted Sunset Shimmer.

"But you'll also totally notice I'm there and it will keep your mind off other things that might be bothering you." Starlight Glimmer was eager to please. If only Sunset would say yes for sure. "So?" she asked expectantly. "What do you think? Can I go back with you?"

Oh, Sunset Shimmer wished she hadn't missed Twilight Sparkle. What should she do? Would it be okay? She just didn't know.

CHAPTER

4

Smirks and Smiles

✶ ✶ ✶

Rarity had *promised* her friends she had a plan to make enough money to repair Camp Everfree. So she'd gone to the mall to walk around. She was sipping a smoothie. "Oh pish," she said to herself. "Three hours and still no ideas for a really spectacular and also lucrative last-minute fund-raiser. Usually window-shopping inspires me."

But they'd already had a fashion show and a gala and a concert...and what else was there? A catchy tune blaring out of a nearby video monitor caught her attention. "Are you a musician?" asked a voice.

Rarity nodded. She was. She played the keytar for the Sonic Rainbooms.

"Do you and your friends love to dance? Are you unique, cool, and stylish?"

Rarity nodded vigorously. "Yes, yes, yes, and obviously!"

"Do you want to win a *cash prize*?"

"*Yes!*" shouted Rarity out loud. This was amazing, a total stroke of luck. It was like magic! Maybe it *was* magic!

The voice continued. "Then follow your dreams and enter the Canterlot Mall Chance to Prance Competition. All you need to enter is a music video of your own original song and dance. Then *you* could be dancin' your way to first prize! Sign up now at the booth near the Aunt Orange smoothie kiosk."

Rarity was right there! How come she hadn't noticed the pile of entry forms earlier? She took one, grabbed a pen from her purse, and began filling it out. Already she could see her friends dancing their way to victory. How hard could this be? They were sure to win!

"Rarity! What a nice surprise!" It was Sunny Flare with all her friends from Crystal Prep. Sunny Flare had a completed entry form in her hands.

"Sour Sweet! Sunny Flare!" Rarity smiled. "Why, it's been ages."

"It's only been three weeks since the

Friendship Games," noted Sugarcoat with a raised eyebrow.

Rarity laughed awkwardly. "Is that all? Wow! How is everything over at Crystal Prep Academy?"

"Things at CPA have never been better," explained Sunny Flare.

"Yeah," Sour Sweet bragged. "We're going to have the spring dance on a yacht!"

"Sounds divine!" said Rarity.

"Are you signing up for the Chance to Prance contest, too?" Lemon Zest asked.

"I am," answered Rarity. She pushed her entry form through the slot of a wooden box. Done. Now she and her friends were committed.

"We definitely aren't here because we just like standing in lines." Lemon Zest smirked. "I assume you already have a video concept figured out? The competition is going to be pret-ty fierce."

"Yes, obviously, of course we do!" said Rarity instantly.

Only she didn't really. And now she realized that winning the competition might not be so easy after all. Thank goodness she didn't have to solve this problem all by herself. It was time to head to the music room. Maybe one of the other girls would have a plan.

CHAPTER

5

Giggles and Groans

★ ★ ★

Everyone was in the music room when Rarity finally arrived. Everyone, that is, except for Sunset Shimmer. Where was she? She wasn't usually late.

But Rarity couldn't wait to tell everyone her wonderful plan. She was bursting with excitement. "See? We'll write some lyrics for our new song and we'll choreograph some dance moves. Then our video will win the cash prize! And voilà!"

Applejack's brow was furrowed with concern. "You make it sound easy as pie—"

"That's because it is!" interrupted Rarity enthusiastically. "Even the Crystal Prep girls agree."

Now Twilight was worried. "They do?"

"Is that a problem, darling?" asked Rarity. Twilight Sparkle had transferred from Crystal Prep to Canterlot High just after the Friendship Games. She hadn't been happy there.

"Oh no," Twilight rushed to reassure her. "It's not. It's just…"

Spike hopped up beside her. "Well, if you ask me, Crystal Prep has got nothing on CHS! I love it here!"

Fluttershy reached over and scratched him under his chin.

"See what I mean?" Spike's doggy tail was thumping happily.

The girls were all ready to get started choreographing their dance moves when Rarity brought up one other teeny-tiny little thing she'd forgotten to mention. "I would need to use our fund-raiser money to buy costume materials for the video."

"Hmmm," said Rainbow Dash thoughtfully. "How much is the grand prize worth?"

"More than double what we need to fix up Camp Everfree!"

"Pssh!" Rainbow Dash grinned. "Then of course you can use the money for costumes!"

Applejack agreed. "What the hay? Why not?" She handed Rarity the cashbox.

Twilight Sparkle was busily punching numbers into her calculator. "According to my calculations," she told the others, "if we lend Rarity the funds we've already raised, we stand to gain four times as much money as we have now."

"Sweet!" gushed Rainbow Dash.

"But," Twilight continued, "if we lose the video contest, we'll be completely back to square one—and zero dollars. We won't have any way of repairing Camp Everfree. Anyone else think this is an awfully risky endeavor?"

Everyone was thinking the same thing. Maybe it wasn't the best idea, but it was their only idea. Twilight looked from one girl to the other. "I m-mean," she stuttered, "me neither."

Rarity beamed proudly. "All right, girls,

who's ready to shoot our winning dance music video?"

"Yeah!"

"All right!"

"Let's go!"

"Now all we need is a concept!" said Rarity. That was the other teensy-weensy thing she hadn't mentioned. They needed a winning idea.

The whole room was instantly silent.

"Do you think we can pull this off in so little time?" worried Twilight Sparkle again.

Rainbow Dash glared at her. "Are you crazy? We're great at doing stuff superfast. Just look at Pinkie Pie. While we've been talking, she's been building a castle made entirely out of chocolate bars."

Pinkie Pie was positioning the last bar against her chocolate castle to create a drawbridge. She grinned at the other girls and took a bite out of it. "Want some?" she added.

"All I want is a video concept," said Rarity.

"Definitely!" agreed everyone.

"I'm sure if we put our heads together we can come up with something," Applejack added.

Pinkie Pie instantly pressed her forehead against Twilight's. The other girls huddled close.

"I think it's working," Pinkie Pie gushed after an instant.

"Yeah," agreed Applejack. "I got somethin', too!"

Applejack began describing her video concept. All the girls would be wearing overalls and cowboy hats. Instead of guitars and microphones, they'd be holding cookie sheets and rolling pins. "So we're in home ec class, bakin' some apple fritters," she told the others.

Rarity shrieked despite herself. Overalls? Never!

"And then a fresh batch comes outta the fryer," Applejack continued. "And everybody's havin' a great time!"

"Wait." Rarity scratched her head, trying to imagine all this as a dance routine. "So basically we're eating pastries at school in our music video?"

Applejack's stomach growled and she grinned. "Oh, I guess I'm just kinda hungry."

Rarity shook her head. "Anyone have another idea?"

"Oh, I do!" Rainbow Dash jumped in. "So...we're in the middle of a jungle! And we're being chased by henchmen who are shooting poison arrows at us. When suddenly, out of nowhere, the shadow of a beast appears!"

"Wait a second," interrupted Twilight Sparkle. "Isn't this a scene from the latest Daring Do book?"

Rainbow Dash blushed. Daring Do was her favorite series. She'd read every book. That's why she'd written a fan letter to the director working on the movie when she found out he was an alumnus of Camp Everfree. But maybe it wasn't the best idea for a dance routine. "Oh well," she admitted. "That's why it seemed like a cool idea. Never mind."

"Okay!" Pinkie was jumping up and down. "I've got it!"

Rarity smiled hesitantly. She wasn't so sure. "Tell us."

"We'll start out on"—she paused for dramatic effect—"the moon!"

No one said a word.

"We'll be wearing really sparkly costumes," Pinkie Pie reassured the others, but when they didn't respond, she had an even better idea. "No! Wait! We'll be wearing space suits! And we'll be surrounded by gorgonzola cheese. But then, a space doggie will walk over and start to eat the cheese!"

Spike's tail was wagging. "*Mmm!* Rich with buttery undertones," he barked.

"*Stop!*" Rarity was clenching her fists and her face was red.

Pinkie Pie's face fell with disappointment. "Aww, why not?"

"Because the contest is for dance music videos, and not one of your ideas included dancing at all!"

"But they were pretty funny, huh?" Pinkie Pie grinned. "I liked yours, Rainbow Dash. I love Daring Do, too!"

"Thanks, Pinkie!"

Rarity screeched with frustration.

"Are you okay?" asked Fluttershy.

"Okay?" Rarity looked like she was about to explode. "The contest deadline is tomorrow. We don't have any time and we've been wasting it."

She stormed out of the room in a huff.

Nobody knew what to say. After all, they had tried.

CHAPTER

6

Hooves and Helping Hands

★ ★ ★

Sunset Shimmer landed on the grass in front of the Wondercolt. An instant later, Starlight Glimmer followed.

Starlight Glimmer staggered dizzily to her feet. "What happened?" She gave a little whinny that sounded more like a shudder.

A group of students walking by stared at them.

"Hi!" Sunset Shimmer waved to them. In a hushed voice she whispered to Starlight Glimmer, "It's all pretty weird at first, but try to roll with it."

Starlight Glimmer was staring down at her body, baffled. She was wiggling her fingers. "Are these...?"

"Hands," explained Sunset Shimmer.

"And what happened to the rest of my hooves—"

"Feet!" Sunset Shimmer interrupted. "Those are feet. Remember the whole thing where I said you'd need to lay low? Now would be a good time to play it cool."

"Right." Starlight Glimmer nodded. She ran her fingers through her long hair. It felt strangely soft. "Play it cool." She dropped down on all fours and began awkwardly staggering forward.

A kid walking past snickered. Sunset Shimmer quickly pulled Starlight Glimmer to her feet.

Starlight Glimmer blushed, embarrassed. She realized that everyone else was walking on their legs. Legs. Feet. Arms. Hands. She was trying to adjust to the strange sensation of having a human body.

Just then Sunset Shimmer caught sight of Rarity. She looked very upset. "Is everything all right?" she asked her friend.

"Since you asked...the answer is *no*!" She plopped down on the grass and put her head in her hands.

She didn't notice Starlight Glimmer. Sunset Shimmer held her finger to her lips, instructing the new girl to be quiet.

"What's happening?" Sunset Shimmer wanted to know.

"I came up with the perfect idea for a fund-raiser! It landed in my lap like magic. The mall is sponsoring a video contest and all we have to do is dance and sing, and then we can win enough money to make the repairs to the camp, but nobody can agree on a concept for our video and the deadline is tomorrow! Everybody wants to do something different! But the worst part is that the Crystal Prep girls are entering, too, and everyone knows how competitive they are, so they'll probably win and we'll never get to go back to Camp Everfree."

"Whoa!" said Starlight Glimmer.

Rarity blinked in confusion, just noticing the girl sitting beside Sunset Shimmer.

"Rarity, this is Starlight Glimmer. She's new."

"Hi!" said Rarity politely.

Starlight Glimmer smiled. "Why can't everyone do something different in your dance?"

"What?" Rarity didn't know what she was talking about.

"You said that everybody was doing something different. Maybe they should. Maybe that's what would make your dance special."

Rarity's face lit up. "You're right! Each member of the Rainbooms could dance in a different style—like flamenco, hip-hop, or street ballet. That way everyone could do what they do best! And we'll wear costumes to match each genre! Designed by yours truly, of course . . . I'd better run to the fabric store before it closes. And thank you . . ."

"Starlight Glimmer," she said, smiling.

"Maybe you'd like to join us..." Rarity suggested.

"I'm kind of all hooves." Starlight Glimmer blushed.

"All hooves?" Rarity laughed. "Sounds like you've got just the right moves! We've been known to do a little ponying ourselves." She winked at Sunset Shimmer.

But Sunset Shimmer didn't notice. She was distracted. She had just seen a wispy trail of magic seeping out from behind the Wondercolt statue. Magic was leaking into their world from Equestria. But where would it go? What could it do?

She had to find some way to keep an eye on it—without worrying her friends. After all, they had enough to think about. They had to repair Camp Everfree.

CHAPTER 7

Twirls and Swirls

★ ★ ★

Rarity was sitting in a director's chair. She had set up a camera on a tripod and was wearing a sparkly disco dress. "Let's take it from the top one more time," she told everyone. "Rainbow Dash, don't forget your cue. It's when Fluttershy does her triple pirouette, okay?" She clicked the play button and took her place.

Fluttershy flexed her ballet slippers. Rainbow Dash hopped in her sneakers. Applejack clogged around in her boots.

Sunset Shimmer began to sing, *"There's a stirring in my soles. There's a rhythm taking hold!"* She twirled like a flamenco dancer and swirled her long skirt.

"Sparkles all across the room. We've got on our dancing shoes!" trilled Twilight Sparkle.

Fluttershy executed a perfect triple pirouette and Rainbow Dash went into a break-dancing spin. It was electric!

Starlight Glimmer was watching from the sidelines. *"Neigh! Neigh! Neigh!"* she exclaimed, clapping wildly. Sunset Shimmer gave her a pointed look. *"Yay! Yay! Yay!"* she corrected herself.

"We want to see you bust a move!" encouraged Rarity.

Starlight Glimmer pranced onto the stage. She lifted her knees and galloped a little in a circle. She was just being herself. It was getting a lot easier to act like a human being.

"Love it!" shouted Rarity. Applejack and Pinkie Pie began imitating her. Now all the girls were in a line, perfectly synchronized. *"We've got different styles, but we dance to the same beat,"* they sang.

Everyone joined in. *"It's Dance Magic. When we spin or when we slide, doing kicks from side to side. It's a thrilling kind of ride. It's Dance Magic! When we snap or when we sway, dancing all our cares away! Yeah, that's what we're here to say!"*

All the girls took a bow.

"That was amazing!" gushed Starlight Glimmer.

Rarity clicked off the video recorder. "Thanks to you and your great suggestion, Starlight Glimmer. I'm glad you are visiting Canterlot High."

"Do you think we'll win the Chance to Prance contest?" wondered Fluttershy out loud.

Rarity's face fell. That was the question, wasn't it? They were taking a big risk. They'd spent all their money on the costumes. Now they would have to send in their video and wait for the results. "I hope we've saved Camp Everfree," she said.

"We've done the best we can," whispered Fluttershy. "Right, Sunset Shimmer?"

But Sunset Shimmer was distracted. She'd seen another wispy trail of magic slide under the door and dissolve. Where was it going? That was the last thing they needed right now…magic trouble.

"There's no guarantee we're going to win." Rarity sighed.

All the girls looked downcast—except for Rainbow Dash.

Rainbow Dash looked like she was about to burst. She had a big announcement. "Well, even if we don't win the contest, I have a backup plan!"

"You do?"

"Really?"

"What is it?" Everyone wanted to know. They crowded around Rainbow Dash. This was amazing.

She was grinning from ear to ear. "Remember how I told you I wrote Canter Zoom, the director of the Daring Do movie?"

The girls nodded—except for Starlight Glimmer, who looked confused.

"Daring Do is the same adventure series you know, but here it's being turned into a movie," Sunset Shimmer whispered to her.

"Well," continued Rainbow Dash, "he's really happy we're helping out Camp Everfree—"

"And he wants to pay for the deposit and all the repairs and we don't have to worry about anything anymore?" Pinkie Pie interrupted, clapping her hands.

"Not exactly," said Rainbow Dash. "But he has invited us to visit the set of the new Daring Do movie."

"Wow!"

"That's so cool!"

"And maybe…" Rainbow Dash continued. "He can put us in his movie and make us stars and we won't ever have to worry about Camp Everfree ever again!" Pinkie Pie exclaimed enthusiastically, accidentally touching the geode around her neck. A spray of pink sparkles wafted through the air around her.

"Something like that." Rainbow Dash smiled. "Or we might just find a way to be helpful on the set and he'll want to help *us* out."

"I like the sound of that," said Applejack.

"And at least it will keep our minds off the dance-video competition until the results are in." Rarity nodded.

The only one who didn't seem happy was Sunset Shimmer. Her brow was furrowed, and she kept glancing around the room. As they were packing up their things, Starlight Glimmer noticed that Sunset Shimmer was distracted. "You're really worried about saving your camp, aren't you?" she asked her new friend.

"I am," Sunset Shimmer admitted. "But it's more than that. There's Equestria magic on the loose here now. I saw another wisp of it while we were performing. I feel like I need to keep an eye on it and make sure nothing bad happens. Magic doesn't work here the same way it does back in Equestria. Any number of terrible things could happen. I probably shouldn't go to the movie set."

Starlight Glimmer nodded. She was thinking. She wanted to help out her new friends. "What if I investigated it for you? After all, the best person to handle Equestria magic is someone from Equestria! Right?"

"You'd do that?"

"Of course. Besides, back in Equestria, we love Daring Do as a *book* series. Going to the *movie* set doesn't mean that much to me. I'll let you know if I see anything suspicious. Okay?"

"It's a deal!" said Sunset Shimmer. "You know what?"

"What?" Starlight Glimmer asked.

"You are kind of a natural at this friend-ship thing."

Starlight Glimmer blushed. Because that was the best thing of all to hear.

CHAPTER

8

Lights, Camera, and Action

✦ ✦ ✦

A flash of lightning illuminated a volcano glowing with molten lava. A cloaked figure shook the rain from his face and raised his staff in the air menacingly. "It is almost time," he cackled. "Once I have all three relics, no one will be able to stop me, and Marapore will fall! For I am the Stalwart Stallion—"

"Whoa!" squealed Rainbow Dash. "Whoa! Whoa! *Whoa!*"

"Cut!" yelled the director, Canter Zoom.

The rain abruptly stopped. The lights glared on. The actor playing the Stalwart Stallion looked irritated. Canter Zoom glared at the girls sitting to the side, watching the Daring Do movie being filmed.

"Sorry," Rainbow Dash apologized. "But at this point in the story, *the Stalwart Stallion* would be known as *Mojo*."

The girls were all embarrassed. They squirmed in their seats. They were trying to be as polite as possible. After all, it was a big deal just being allowed on the set.

"What?" exclaimed Rainbow Dash. "You think he wants Daring Do fans to call him out for making a mistake like that?"

Canter Zoom took in what she'd said.

He'd been irritated, it was true, but maybe it was a good point after all. "Let's go again," he instructed the film crew. "And this time say *Mojo* instead of *the Stalwart Stallion*."

Rainbow Dash grinned triumphantly. Their plan was to help out, after all, and she was already jumping in.

When the scene wrapped, the girls let Canter Zoom know how much they appreciated the invitation.

"I can't believe we're really here," gushed Rainbow Dash.

"Thank you so much for letting us come, Mr. Zoom," said Twilight Sparkle nicely.

"We promise we won't get in the way." Sunset Shimmer glared at Rainbow Dash. "Again."

Canter Zoom smiled warmly at the girls. "As a fellow Camp Everfree alum, I was more than happy to afford the girls who helped save it the chance to visit the set of our little film."

"*Little?*" scoffed Rainbow Dash. "This is Daring Do we're talking about. This movie is gonna be huge!"

Canter Zoom beamed, but before he could say anything, a production assistant interrupted him with a problem. "They can't find the costume Daring Do is supposed to wear in the nightclub scene!" she fretted.

Canter Zoom took a deep breath. He looked very worried. "If we are ever able to finish it, it will be." He excused himself.

Twilight looked over a printout. "According to our visitor schedules, they won't start shooting the next scene for a while, which means we have time to—"

"Get a great picture taken next to *the*

Chestnut Magnifico," Rarity interrupted. "The actress playing Daring Do!"

Fluttershy clapped her hands. "Ask her to sign my petition to bring more bird feeders to Canterlot High!"

Spike was confused and scratched his head with his paw. The other girls looked at Fluttershy, bewildered.

"Chestnut is a really avid supporter of a foundation that helps build homes for animals in need," explained Fluttershy.

"Oh, okay," said Twilight, still not convinced. "But I was thinking that we could—"

"Check out all the sets," Sunset Shimmer interrupted her. She took a quick glance at her phone. No messages from Starlight Glimmer. Maybe everything would be fine. There probably wouldn't be anything to worry about.

"I'd sure like to get a closer look at that volcano," agreed Applejack.

"Actually," insisted Twilight, who wanted to remind everyone why they'd come to the set in the first place, "I thought that we would—"

"Find the buffet!" Spike barked.

"And the cupcake fountain!" squealed Pinkie Pie.

A cupcake fountain? What was that? "I don't know what a cupcake fountain is," admitted Rainbow Dash. "But I'm pretty sure that they don't have one."

Pinkie Pie laughed. She pulled a brochure out of her backpack. "Of course they do. I read it in my *100 Things You Didn't Know About This Movie Studio: Insider's Tour Guide*."

"Is the number-one thing we didn't know

that the guy who founded this studio was an eccentric oddball with a sweet tooth?" Applejack asked sarcastically.

"*Yes!*" affirmed Pinkie Pie, holding up her guide.

"I guess we're splitting up." Twilight smiled indulgently. Leave it to Pinkie Pie to find the cupcakes. But she wanted to keep an eye on their plan to repair Camp Everfree. If they lost the contest, they'd have no money left and no time to make any more. Maybe Canter Zoom would reward Rainbow Dash for being such a good fact-checker. Twilight turned to her friend. "I don't suppose you want to—"

"Check out the props designed especially for the movie?"

"You read my mind!" said Twilight.

If there was one thing wrong with them, Rainbow Dash would be sure to notice.

CHAPTER

9

Clues and Calamities

★ ★ ★

Rarity and Fluttershy found Chestnut Magnifico's trailer, but Fluttershy hung back, too nervous to knock on the door.

"Maybe . . . we shouldn't bother her," Fluttershy murmured.

"Darling, please." Rarity sighed. "Actresses love interacting with their fans."

The door flew open and an obviously furious movie star stormed past the girls.

"Miss Magnifico," Rarity called.

But the movie star was yelling into her cell phone. "I don't care if I'm under contract! This is a joke, and I want this film shut down, do you hear me?"

She sailed past the girls without even seeming to notice them. Fluttershy and Rarity felt embarrassed. Maybe they shouldn't bother her. But what did it mean that she didn't want to be in the Daring Do movie? That couldn't be good! Maybe there was some way they could help.

Meanwhile, Sunset Shimmer and Applejack were exploring the set.

Applejack was impressed with how realistic it was. "Wonder how long it takes to build somethin' like this."

"Several weeks, I'd bet," guessed Sunset Shimmer.

"They sure do go all out makin' it look like the real deal."

Sunset Shimmer noticed a crumpled candy wrapper near the base of the volcano. "Though I don't think the rain forest is known for its...Bon Mot peanut butter praline crunch bars."

"Pocket that," said Applejack. "Wouldn't want it ruining the shot."

Sunset Shimmer nodded. There were a lot of ways they could lend a hand on the set. Maybe one of them would make a real difference. Maybe Canter Zoom would remark on how helpful they were.

She felt her phone ping in her pocket. It was a message from Starlight Glimmer.

I saw one wisp of magic, that's all, and it

disappeared in the cafeteria. But I am making so many new friends. DJ Pon-3 and I are going to the Sweet Shoppe this afternoon!

Great, Sunset Shimmer texted her back. *We are having fun, too.*

In another corner of the set, Rainbow Dash and Twilight were walking in a make-believe marketplace. There was a stonelike statue of the Stalwart Stallion. At its base was a treasure chest.

Rainbow Dash peeked inside, thrilled. "Wow! These are the three magical relics! The Sword!"

"The Staff!" Twilight Sparkle pointed at it.

They gazed speechlessly in wonder at the third, the Arrow. The props were exactly as they had imagined. They were perfect.

"And you can't forget the Arrow!" ordered a voice.

Rainbow Dash and Twilight Sparkle whirled around and found themselves face-to-face with a freckle-faced girl not much older than they were.

She wrinkled her nose. "You're from Canterlot High, right?"

The girls nodded.

"I'm Juniper Montage," she introduced herself. "Canter the director's niece. What do you think of the props?" She gestured toward the relics in the treasure chest.

"They're awesome!" enthused Rainbow Dash.

"A. K. Yearling is very hands-on when it comes to the sets and props for the movie," Juniper explained.

"Have you ever met her?" asked Twilight.

A. K. Yearling was the author of the Daring Do series.

"Just once when she came to check out the relics. I did get her to sign a copy of the latest book in the series, though."

Rainbow Dash and Twilight were very impressed.

"So what do you do here?" asked Twilight.

Juniper smiled shyly. "Mostly I bring my uncle coffee and help get everything ready for shooting. I've been on set for all the movies he's shot here. Pretty much know every inch of this place like the back of my hand." She laughed. "I tried to convince him to cast *me* as Daring Do, but he didn't really go for that."

Neither girl was sure how to respond. Daring Do was a big part for a famous actress. Was this girl joking? Probably.

"Hey!" Juniper said. "Have you guys seen the set for Caballeron's secret lair?"

Rainbow Dash and Twilight shook their heads, but their eyes were wide with excitement.

"They usually lock the door to that set," explained Juniper. "But I've got keys that open just about every door in the place." She chuckled self-importantly. "Come on. I'll show you."

And off they went, hurrying right past Spike and Pinkie Pie, who had discovered a buffet table. They were covered in crumbs.

Pinkie Pie was very concerned. They'd found three different buffet tables, six different kinds of fondue, two rooms filled with candy, but no cupcake fountain. Maybe it didn't exist after all. "Oh well." Pinkie Pie sighed. "At least we found those peanut butter praline crunch bars! They weren't in my guidebook, but they sure were delicious."

Spike patted his stomach in agreement. "I'll say. You think they've got any more?"

Before Pinkie Pie could answer, a furious Chestnut Magnifico strode into the room, with Canter Zoom, frazzled and unhappy, trailing after her.

"One more month, Chestnut," the director begged the movie star. "That's all we need."

Chestnut shook her head dramatically. She surveyed the buffet, looking for something to nibble.

"I'm doing everything I can to keep us on schedule," Canter told her. "But with all the setbacks we've had, I just don't think we can do it. If you could agree to stay for one more—"

"Unacceptable!" screamed Chestnut at the top of her lungs. She looked back at the buffet, even angrier than she was before. "And where are my imported peanut butter praline crunch bars?"

Spike gulped. "Now would probably be a good time to resume the search for the cupcake fountain," he whispered to Pinkie Pie conspiratorially.

Together, they slunk out of the room. Making trouble for Canter was not a good idea…and it looked like they just had. All of a sudden this wasn't feeling like a very good plan for restoring Camp Everfree.

When filming was about to begin again, the girls were buzzing with all they had seen.

"You guys should've seen the relics. They

were amazing!" whispered Rainbow Dash to her friends.

"Quiet on the set!" shouted Canter Zoom, exasperated. *"Please!"*

"Sorry!" apologized Rainbow Dash. But she leaped out of her seat to take one more peek at the relics in their treasure chest.

"And action!" Canter Zoom bellowed.

Thunder boomed and lightning crackled. The villain again approached the volcano. It began to shiver and shake. Was it about to explode? Or fall apart?

"That doesn't look right," noted Applejack. "Should it be shaking like that?"

Twilight was confused, too. "No, the volcano is supposed to be still until after the villain performs his magic!"

"Will you please just watch the scene?" begged Rarity. Movies were always different from the books they were based on. Why couldn't the other girls accept that?

The volcano was rumbling like an out-of-control washing machine. A piece near the top fell off, revealing the wires underneath. Another piece fell off. Lights and camera equipment began toppling over.

"Ahhhhh!" screamed Canter Zoom. "Cut! Cut! Cut!"

Something was seriously the matter with this production. But what?

CHAPTER

10

Mishaps and Mysteries

★ ★ ★

The entire set was in shambles. The volcano would need to be rebuilt. Canter Zoom was so upset. He sat in his director's chair, his head in his hands. "What is going on around here? We just filmed on this volcano yesterday and it was fine. This could set us back weeks!"

Rainbow Dash appeared, out of breath and as upset as the director. "They're gone! All gone!" she shouted.

Canter Zoom was confused. "What's gone?"

"The relics!" Juniper Montage was right beside Rainbow Dash. Everyone rushed over to the other set. They stared in shock at the empty chest at the foot of the statue.

"I wanted to check them out again up close," explained Rainbow Dash, "and they weren't there."

Canter Zoom was beside himself with frustration. "This can't be happening," he moaned. "What are we going to do?"

"Couldn't you just get the prop department to make new ones?" Sunset Shimmer suggested.

Canter Zoom sighed. "The missing relics

were personally approved by A. K. Yearling. We could have new ones made, but we can't use them until Miss Yearling has given them her official stamp of approval. You'd think it would be easy to reach someone who is always holed up in her office writing, but Miss Yearling is a very difficult woman to track down."

"It'll be okay, though, right?" Rainbow Dash was trying to be optimistic.

But Canter Zoom couldn't hear it. He was defeated. "Chestnut's contract with us is almost up, and with the volcano collapsing and now this...I fear we'll have to stop production altogether."

The girls couldn't believe what they were hearing.

"But you have to finish this movie!" exclaimed Rainbow Dash. "Think of all the

Daring Do fans who'll be disappointed if you don't."

"Are you sure there's nothing you can do?" asked Twilight Sparkle.

A huge crash was the answer. Something else had collapsed.

"I'm so sorry." Canter sighed. "Please excuse me." He raced back to the other set to see what was going on.

Twilight bit her lip. Something wasn't right, but what was it? "There was trouble with one of the costumes when we first arrived. A set that was fine yesterday just collapsed. And now the most important props in the movie have been stolen," she said, thinking out loud. "I don't think these are just coincidences."

"Me neither," agreed Sunset Shimmer. "All the things that have gone wrong on set have put production on hold. It seems to me like someone is going to a lot of trouble to make sure this movie doesn't get made."

Spike growled. "Who would want to—"

A gasp from Fluttershy interrupted him. "Oh dear! You don't think…" Her voice trailed off. She couldn't say it.

"Certainly not!" said Rarity, guessing what she was thinking.

Fluttershy filled in the others. "When Rarity and I followed Chestnut Magnifico to her trailer, we overheard her saying something about shutting down the movie…."

Rarity rushed to the movie star's defense. "She said she wanted *something* shut down. We don't know that she was talking about the movie."

"Maybe she's just really mad that they're always running out of her imported peanut butter praline crunch bars," suggested Pinkie Pie.

Sunset Shimmer pulled the crumpled wrapper she'd found out of her pocket. "Bon Mot peanut butter praline crunch bars?"

"Those are the ones!" said Pinkie Pie excitedly.

Spike covered his face with his paw. "We may have tried a few ourselves."

But Sunset Shimmer was making some connections. "We found this wrapper on the volcano set right before it collapsed!"

Twilight nodded in agreement. "It sure seems like all signs are pointing to Chestnut Magnifico as the one causing all the problems around here."

"I don't know who's behind this," interjected Rainbow Dash. "Or what's going on, but the first thing we need to do is find those relics. The sooner we do, the less likely they'll have to shut down production for good."

That seemed like a sensible plan. Twilight Sparkle agreed. "The relics were here earlier, and if Chestnut is behind this..."

Rarity scoffed in disbelief. Why would a movie star ruin her own movie?

But Twilight ignored her and continued. "Then they must still be around here somewhere."

"Chestnut Magnifico is a very highly acclaimed actress!" exclaimed Rarity. "She'd never do something this dramatic!"

"An actress? Dramatic?" Sunset Shimmer mocked. "Never!"

"She might do something like this if she was trying to get out of working on a movie she didn't want to do," suggested Applejack.

Sunset Shimmer had a plan. "Why don't Fluttershy, Pinkie Pie, Spike, and I follow Chestnut Magnifico and see if we can find anything out?"

"Let's do it! C'mon!" Pinkie Pie squealed as she started to run off. It would be an adventure.

"In the meantime," Twilight suggested to the other girls, "we should look for the relics."

"Where do we even start?" wondered Applejack. "It's not like there's some mysterious, thievin', cloaked figure we can chase after and say, 'Tell us where you're keepin' the relics!'"

Rarity frowned. She held up her hand, pointing.

A cloaked figure was sneaking behind one of the set pieces.

"Hey!" called out Rainbow Dash. "Stop right there!"

Startled, the cloaked figure whirled around for an instant before speeding off in the opposite direction.

Rainbow Dash met everyone's eyes. The chase was on! She touched her geode. It was time for a little superpowered running!

Ten minutes later, the rest of the girls caught up with Rainbow Dash. She was out of breath. "I can't believe I lost them!" She gasped. "My geode gives me super speed, but I guess being awesomely fast isn't all that helpful when the person you are chasing knows their way around better than you do."

Sunset Shimmer caught up with the others. She looked defeated.

"I thought you were followin' Chestnut?" Applejack asked.

Sunset Shimmer's face fell. "We couldn't find her."

"But"—Pinkie Pie giggled—"we did find the cupcake fountain!" She pulled two cupcakes out of her purse and handed one to Spike.

Sunset Shimmer shook her head. "Then we got lost and somehow ended up here. What have you guys been doing?"

"We spotted a super-suspicious cloaked figure but they got away," explained Rainbow Dash. She peered into the corners. They couldn't have gone far. They had to be here somewhere. But where?

A nervous production assistant hurried over to them. "There you are!" she said. "Where are your costumes?"

"Costumes?" Fluttershy was confused.

"We have got to hurry," insisted the

production assistant angrily. "I'm so gonna be fired if you aren't ready. The director wants to shoot in three minutes!"

What was happening? How had they ended up getting parts in the Daring Do movie? No one knew, but they all had to admit—it was pretty exciting!

CHAPTER

11

Dashes Chases

✶ ✶ ✶

The girls arrived back on the set dressed as Power Ponies, all except for Sunset Shimmer, who had somehow gotten the part of the Mane-iac.

"I think there's been some kind of mistake," said Applejack. They didn't know what their lines were. No one had told them what to do.

But no one was listening to her.

"Action!" called Canter Zoom, and the cameras began to roll. "Wait." He stopped a moment later. "Who are these girls?"

"They're the Power Ponies," explained the production assistant.

Canter Zoom shook his head. He looked like he was about to explode.

"I'm fired, aren't I?" said the production assistant in a soft voice.

"You are *so* fired," confirmed Canter Zoom.

"Hey!" Applejack called out. She pointed at the cloaked figure disappearing behind a set piece.

The girls and Spike raced after the figure. They ran from movie set to movie set, hurrying past old castles, across racetracks, and hurling themselves over the hoods of cars. They chased the cloaked figure through a desolate planet in outer space. Directors and lighting technicians yelled at them, but they didn't stop. They had to catch the cloaked figure. This was how they could save Canter Zoom's movie—and maybe Camp Everfree. But they could not catch up. The figure disappeared again, and the girls didn't know where to go next. At last, they sat down, utterly exhausted.

They were on the set of what looked like an ordinary downtown street—except that there were large buckets of what looked like chocolate pudding.

"What's this place supposed to be?" wondered Applejack.

Rainbow Dash sighed, peering into every corner. "And where did they go?"

"They must be around here somewhere," said Twilight, confused. "Wherever *here* is."

Pinkie Pie licked chocolate off her finger. "Are you kidding? This is the set of *Stormy with a Side of Pudding*!"

Applejack scratched her head. "Stormy with a side of *what*, now?"

"It's my all-time favorite movie!" Pinkie Pie exclaimed.

The other girls looked at her blankly. They'd never heard of it.

"I've tried to get you all to watch it, like, a gazillion times," said Pinkie Pie, exasperated. "I've heard they use real pudding…" She licked her finger again. "And now I *know* they do!"

Rainbow Dash was frustrated. "Ugh! We're running out of time. We're supposed to be hunting down the missing relics and catching the bad guy, not eating pudding! If we don't win the dance video contest, this is our only backup plan."

Everyone was so focused on Rainbow Dash that nobody noticed the shadow of a figure moving closer to them.

"We're trying." Twilight Sparkle sighed. "Maybe we should make our way back to the *Daring Do* set. There might have been some clues we missed."

But it was too late.

The cloaked figure was right behind them...with a large net! *"Ahh!"* screamed Sunset Shimmer.

The figure threw it over the girls—but Rarity instinctively touched the geode she wore around her neck, and a protective diamond dome encased the girls. They didn't get entangled in the ropes.

Rainbow Dash didn't wait an instant when Rarity dissolved the dome.

"Don't worry; I've got this," she shouted to her friends. She raced off after the cloaked figure, knocking over a bucket of chocolate pudding in her path. She zoomed at top speed from one set to another. She screeched to a halt in an abandoned lot.

"I saw you come in here. Where are you?" she said to herself.

She heard the soft thud of a footstep and then the quietest of creaks. At the other end of the room was the door to a closet. It was slightly ajar. Very cautiously, Rainbow Dash tiptoed toward it. She slipped inside. Mops and brooms and buckets. Some bottles of cleaning solvents. Stacks of paper towels. And a costume.

Rainbow Dash studied it. She'd seen it

before. "Hey! This is just like the outfit Daring Do wears in the nightclub scene. What's it doing in here?"

But before she could go ask her friends, the closet door shut behind her—and locked.

Rainbow Dash tried to jiggle the handle, but the door wouldn't budge. She was trapped! She pounded on the door. "Hello? Anybody out there?" There was no answer, but at least she had her phone. Except she didn't. With a groan, she discovered that she didn't get any signal in the closet.

Rainbow Dash pounded on the door again and screamed at the top of her lungs. "Help! Help! I'm trapped in here!"

But no one knew where she was.

CHAPTER

12

Pudding and Pie

★ ★ ★

Rainbow Dash had run so fast that none of the girls knew where she was. But they knew they had to find her.

Rarity was worried. "I simply don't see how we'll do it. As fast as she moves, she could be anywhere on the lot by now."

Sunset Shimmer stared at her, amazed.

"You just used your geode, thank goodness—and I wish I'd brought mine. One touch and I'd be able to see Chestnut's memories and get to the bottom of this whole thing."

Pinkie Pie looked unusually thoughtful. She pointed at the overturned bucket of chocolate pudding—and the chocolate footsteps that led away from it. "See?"

"You're a genius, Pinkie Pie!" Twilight Sparkle exclaimed.

"I know!" Pinkie Pie beamed.

"C'mon; this way," said Sunset Shimmer, already following Rainbow Dash's trail.

Pinkie Pie dipped her finger into one of the buckets again. "For the road!" she told the others.

Unfortunately, with each step, the pudding trail got fainter and fainter. "She must be here somewhere," said Pinkie Pie when she could no longer detect any chocolate at all. They were in the abandoned lot.

"Rainbow Dash? Where are ya?" called Applejack.

"Hello? Is anyone here?" added Twilight Sparkle, facing the opposite direction.

Fluttershy was listening. That's when she heard muffled sounds coming from behind a closed door. She pressed her ear up to the closet. "Hello? Rainbow Dash? Are you in there?"

Bang! Bang! Bang!

Someone was pounding on the door from the other side. A muffled voice shouted, "Yes! Help! I'm locked in!"

"It's okay, Rainbow Dash," Fluttershy reassured her soothingly. "We're here."

Sunset Shimmer quickly assessed the situation. "I'll go find someone with a key," she announced.

Twilight Sparkle stopped her. "Wait." She pulled on the chain around her neck. She was wearing her geode. She held her hand up to the door—and a moment later, the handle turned.

Rarity gasped in amazement. "Did you just make that lock unlock itself?"

"Nice!" Sunset Shimmer grinned.

"I'm thinking maybe we should all start wearing our geodes around," Applejack suggested. "Never know when our new magic might come in handy."

Twilight opened the door and Rainbow Dash burst out of the closet. "Am I happy to see you!"

The girls noticed the costume clutched in her hands.

"How did you find me?" asked Rainbow Dash. "I gave up banging on that door five minutes ago."

"Pudding never lies," said Pinkie Pie without a giggle or a grin.

Sunset Shimmer was looking at the costume. "Is that the dress that went missing when we first got here?"

Rainbow Dash nodded. "Yeah. But I didn't see the person who locked me in, and there's still no sign of the relics."

"I say we head back to the scene of the crime. Maybe there's somethin' there that could lead us to all the relics," Applejack suggested.

But another idea had suddenly occurred

to Twilight Sparkle. "Or we could let the culprit lead us to them!"

"How?" asked Rainbow Dash. "I just told you I didn't see who locked me in."

"I've got a pretty good idea who our thief is," explained Twilight Sparkle as the girls crowded around. "But we're going to need Canter Zoom's help to catch her."

As they were putting together their plan, another text arrived from Starlight Glimmer. *Bad news. I saw wisps of magic at the Sweet Shoppe. They seemed to be disappearing into shiny surfaces—metal, mirrors, that kind of thing. Nothing else to report.*

Sunset Shimmer sighed. They might be on the verge of solving this mystery—but it sounded like there was another waiting for them when they got back to Canterlot High.

CHAPTER

13

Answers and Apologies

★ ★ ★

Canter Zoom studied the missing costume. "You found this in the supply closet?" he asked.

Rainbow Dash nodded. They'd explained everything to him.

"We didn't find the relics," added Twilight Sparkle. "But we don't think the thief has had a chance to take them off the lot yet. We wanted your permission to search the Tricorner Villages set from top to bottom. Maybe we'll find a clue that will lead us to where they're hidden."

"Of course," agreed Canter Zoom, relieved that he might be able to save his movie after all. "I'll help you."

But first he had to see to a few things. He pulled Chestnut Magnifico aside. "I need you to get to hair and makeup," he told the star. "As soon as we get the relics, we're going to start shooting again."

She sniffed, her nose in the air. "We'll see."

Canter Zoom took a big breath, trying to keep his cool. "Juniper," he said to his freckle-faced niece. "Could you do a smoothie run? I'm sure all this sleuthing is going to make everyone thirsty."

"Absolutely!" answered Juniper loudly, jumping up.

No one was left on the movie set. Chestnut had gone to her trailer. Canter Zoom had followed the girls. Juniper was off getting smoothies. That was when the cloaked figure appeared. A hand reached behind a canvas flap and emerged holding...the relics!

The girls jumped out from behind a building. They hadn't left the set after all. They'd set a trap.

The cloaked figure whirled around and her hood fell away. It was Juniper Montage! She dropped the relics, stunned.

"I told you it wasn't Chestnut!" Rarity announced triumphantly.

"Look!" said Juniper Montage, scrambling. "I found the missing relics."

But the girls weren't buying it. "Because you're the one who stole them," Sunset Shimmer accused her.

Canter Zoom couldn't believe it. "She wouldn't," he said, shaking his head.

"She would. And she did," said Twilight Sparkle. "What she didn't expect was for Rainbow Dash to come to the Tricorner set before she was able to sneak them off to a safer hiding place. So she was forced to hide them in the first place she could find."

Twilight explained that the fact that Juniper had admitted she knew "every inch of the studio like the back of her hand" was the first clue. That's how she was always able to find hiding places so that she could sneak up on the girls when she needed to. Plus,

Juniper had also admitted she had keys to "just about every door in the place," including, Twilight pointed out, the closet near the abandoned set.

"When did you figure out it was her?" asked Rainbow Dash.

"I started to piece things together when I unlocked the door to get you out of the supply closet," Twilight revealed. "But I knew Juniper would never admit she was the one who had taken the relics."

"Unless, of course, she was caught in the act of trying to remove them again!" Sunset Shimmer said as she figured it out.

Twilight nodded. "Which is why I told you, Canter Zoom, to send her on that smoothie run. So she'd think she had the opportunity to get the relics off the lot where we'd never find them."

Juniper Montage hung her head in shame. "But instead of searching the Tricorners set, you all secretly followed me here."

"Bingo!" squealed Pinkie Pie.

But there was still something Canter Zoom didn't understand. "Why would you do this?" he asked Juniper.

"I'm sorry! Okay? I'm sorry." She took a big breath. Her plan had failed, and there was nothing left to do but admit it. "I just can't stand Chestnut. She's always eating all the peanut butter praline crunch bars, which are the only candy bars I like...."

Sunset pulled the crumpled candy wrapper out of her pocket. Another clue!

"That's hardly a reason to—" began Canter Zoom.

"And I was mad at you for casting her as Daring Do!" Juniper blurted out. "I mean,

I've told you over and over again how badly I wanted to play Daring Do, and you just ignored me!"

Canter Zoom was even more bewildered. "But, Juniper, you're too young! You don't have any experience."

"I know!" she whined defensively. "But I thought if enough things went wrong, Chestnut would back out of the movie and then maybe you'd give me a chance."

Now Canter Zoom was furious. "Not only did you jeopardize production and endanger the safety of the actors and film crew, but you also lied to me and took advantage of my trust!"

Juniper kicked at the floor. What else could she say? She tried apologizing again, this time a little more sincerely. "I'm sorry. I never meant to hurt anyone, and I was going to return all the props, just as soon as Chestnut quit. I hope you can forgive me."

Canter Zoom sat down heavily in his director's chair. If it hadn't been for the visiting girls from Canterlot High, his entire movie would have been ruined. Still, Juniper was his niece, she was young, and everyone made mistakes. "I can forgive you," he told her, "but I *am* sorry to say you are no longer welcome on the set, and it will be a long time before I consider allowing you back here."

He extended his hand and asked her to return her studio keys.

Chestnut Magnifico chose that moment to make a grand entrance. "Canter, there you are!" she trilled. "So sorry I'm not in makeup, but I've just gotten a call from my agent. I no longer have to work on that ridiculous documentary about nests next month. I swear, when they approached me, I thought they wanted to do a documentary about my organization for homeless animals, not on various nests around the world! Completely misleading! But no matter! That's all behind us!" She waved a hand magnanimously.

Canter Zoom's eyes widened. He might not have to rush the production. "Does this mean...?"

"No more scheduling conflict," confirmed Chestnut. "I can extend my contract and continue filming *Daring Do*!" She caught sight of the missing relics and turned a questioning eye to Canter.

"Yes, they've been found," he said. "And

I don't think we'll have to worry about them disappearing again." He glared at Juniper. She squirmed uncomfortably.

Sunset Shimmer couldn't help but notice that she seemed more upset about getting caught than about having made a mistake. Applejack was right! If only she'd had her geode, she would have been able to find out what Juniper was thinking. But she hadn't.

Twilight Sparkle cleared her throat to catch Canter Zoom's attention.

The director smiled at her appreciatively. "And it's all thanks to our visitors," he acknowledged. "First you save Camp Everfree and now the Daring Do movie. You all are certainly on a roll."

Rainbow Dash couldn't believe it! Her far-out, totally unlikely plan was actually working! "Speaking of roles..." she said.

"Don't suppose you've got any extra parts my friends and I could play? You know, as a reward for saving the day? You wouldn't even have to pay us. You could just pay down the deposit for repairs on Camp Everfree!"

Canter Zoom grinned. "I think we can figure something out."

The girls cheered.

But Juniper Montage looked unhappier than ever. Even without her geode, Sunset Shimmer knew what she was thinking. Juniper Montage was hatching another terrible plan.

CHAPTER

14

Costumes and Credits

✶ ✶ ✶

The camera was rolling. The set was decorated to look like a busy marketplace. Rarity was wearing a vendor's costume and pretending to sell fabric to Sunset Shimmer. Just as Sunset Shimmer held up a piece of cloth, Daring Do raced past them. She nearly bumped into Applejack, who was holding a bushel of apples. Daring Do darted around Pinkie Pie, who was dressed as a street performer, juggling brightly colored pins. She swerved expertly past Twilight, who was carrying a stack of books—and she careered right into Fluttershy.

Daring Do pushed Fluttershy behind her protectively just as the dastardly Stalwart Stallion strode forward.

"You will give me the Sword of Lusitano," he demanded.

"I don't think so," said Chestnut Magnifico as Daring Do.

The Stalwart Stallion cackled devilishly. "Have it your way!" He produced a staff from beneath his cloak and raised it over his head. *"Hostium prohibere!"*

Behind the scenes, the technical experts

sprang into action. The "magic spell" set the ground to rumbling and trembling.

Daring Do hesitated, uncertain what to do next.

"Give up, Daring Do! You can't stop me! The Sword shall be mine!"

But Rainbow Dash, in costume, was ready. She jumped forward and handed Daring Do a whip. Daring Do swung it over her head and cracked it. She knocked the staff out of the Stalwart Stallion's evil hands.

"And . . . *cut!*" yelled Canter Zoom.

The girls cheered. It was a wrap. The movie was done and they were in it, and they had managed to save Camp Everfree and have an adventure at the same time.

"So you'll send in the deposit, right?" said Pinkie Pie to Canter Zoom.

He looked surprised. "After the movie comes out, for sure. But I invested all my money in making it. Now we just have to wait for it to be a success."

The girls' faces fell. It wasn't going to be so easy after all.

"Just like our video!" Rarity sighed. "We did the same thing."

"But you girls can help me! Go to the premiere and tell all your friends about the movie."

"Of course we will," they said.

But after they left, they were more worried than ever.

What if the Daring Do movie wasn't a success? What if they didn't win the dance video contest? What would happen to Camp Everfree then?

And what will happen to the crystal cave where

the geodes came from with so much magic on the loose? wondered Sunset Shimmer. They had to save the camp from disrepair. They just had to. But now the only thing they could do was hope that one of their plans would work.

CHAPTER

15

Mirrors and Magic

★ ★ ★

The dance show sponsoring the contest was playing the videos of all the finalists in the contest on TV. "Dance Magic," the video by the girls at Canterlot High, was in the running. Would it win?

Waiting back at Canterlot High, the girls couldn't believe the good news. Everyone was so excited for them, especially Starlight Glimmer.

"It's a great video," she praised Rarity.

"Thanks to your help." Rarity smiled. "Now, if only we can win."

"Hooves crossed!" said Starlight Glimmer.

Starlight Glimmer still said the strangest things sometimes.

But there was one person who was hoping the girls wouldn't win the dance contest—and that was Juniper Montage.

"Ugh, those girls," she muttered to herself angrily as she passed a television at the mall showing the girls dancing.

Juniper Montage was wearing a simple uniform of black pants with a white shirt and name tag. She was carrying a walkie-talkie, but not because she was a production assistant. Now she was just an usher at the Flixiplex Cinemas. She was still furious about getting caught trying to ruin the Daring Do movie. "First they get me kicked off the set," she fumed. "Now they're about to become stars in their own right!"

She was so preoccupied she nearly bumped right into a poster cutout advertising the *Daring Do* premiere. It was Chestnut Magnifico with the whip raised over her head—and there in the background were the girls in their costumes. Juniper growled with fury. "They're everywhere!"

She kicked over the cardboard advertisement. "I bet they'll be at the premiere tonight," she realized. "I bet I'll be the lucky one ushering them to their seats."

Juniper's walkie-talkie crackled. "Juniper, where are you?" asked an irritated voice.

"We need you back at the popcorn popper stat."

Juniper pretended that she couldn't hear. "What was that?" She crinkled a piece of paper to make it sound like static. "Losing you." She clicked off the walkie-talkie. She needed a break. She was going to go window-shopping around the mall.

If only she didn't have to see those girls dancing on every screen. They were probably going to win the contest. It just wasn't fair. "Tonight would have been about me. I would have been a star!"

She was standing in front of a kiosk selling sunglasses, and she started trying them on. Movie stars always wore sunglasses, and one day, no matter what, she was going to be a movie star. She grabbed a purple pair with frames shaped like big stars. A hand mirror was hanging on a hook, and Juniper grabbed it to get a better look at herself. Did she look like a celebrity? She winced. No. She mostly looked silly.

The bored teenage clerk was watching her and shaking her head, laughing.

"You're right," acknowledged Juniper. "They are a bit much."

She took off the glasses and reached for another pair. She didn't notice that the mirror in her hands was shimmering and sparkling. If Sunset Shimmer were there, she would have known what was happening. She would have spotted the wispy beams of magic seeping in from Equestria to the human world. But Sunset Shimmer wasn't there. And no one else realized what was happening, least of all Juniper Montage.

Juniper was wearing another pair of

sunglasses. She looked at herself in the mirror. She blinked. She looked again. She screamed. She threw the mirror across the hall, terrified.

Staring back at her had not been her own face but the face of a glamorous star, her hair styled, her makeup perfect, her expression grown-up and haughty. It was as if someone had mysteriously touched up her reflection. But how?

"What was that?" she wondered out loud.

Did she dare look in the mirror again? It had landed on the carpet down the hall She picked it up. It was sparkling.

The teenager who had been watching her was distracted, listening to music. She hadn't noticed anything.

Juniper Montage dared to look in the mirror again. There was her reflection—

only more polished and more perfect—blowing her a kiss!

"Incredible!" whispered Juniper Montage.

Without ever taking her hand off the mirror, Juniper reached into her pocket and left a bill on the counter for the teenage clerk. "Keep the change," said Juniper. "Something tells me this thing is worth it."

On her way back to the movie theater, she passed crowds of kids staring down at their phones. But Juniper Montage only had eyes for her magic mirror.

CHAPTER

16

Wishes and Revenge

★ ★ ★

Juniper Montage couldn't pull her eyes away from her enhanced reflection. "It's like this mirror is the only one around here who gets me," she murmured.

Her boss, standing behind her, cleared his throat. He was holding a broom and a dustpan. "Popcorn spill at the condiment counter," he told her.

Juniper just sneered. "Does this look like someone who cleans popcorn spills?" She held up the mirror so her boss could see it.

"No," he answered. "It looks like someone about to fire somebody."

Grumbling, Juniper Montage put the mirror in her pocket and grabbed the broom. She sauntered over to the concession stand and began dragging the broom back and forth. "Ugh, this is the worst," she muttered. "Hey, I know what will perk me up! A little Mirror Me time!"

She took out the mirror and gazed into it with a happy sigh. Her reflected self was posing for the paparazzi and signing autographs. Everyone was looking at her. "That's more like it. Fame. Adoring fans. Everyone clamoring just to be near me."

Her reflection winked at her.

"I wish this popcorn would clean itself so I could just stare at you all day," she said.

It was as if the mirror had heard her. It sparkled. It shimmered. It began to vibrate. It began to make a whirring noise...like a vacuum cleaner. Popcorn was rising up from the floor and disappearing right into the mirror. In an instant, the floor was spotless. The mirror flashed.

"Wow." Juniper's boss said, impressed. "Done already? I'm shocked."

"You and me both!" Juniper agreed, staring at the mirror.

When her boss had walked away, Juniper decided to experiment. She grabbed a box of popcorn and dumped it on the carpet. "Mirror, pick up this popcorn," she commanded.

Nothing happened.

Two moviegoers, arriving for the premiere, tickets in hand, stopped at the concession stand to get some snacks. Juniper completely ignored them and hurtled another handful of popcorn onto the floor.

She gritted her teeth. "Mirror, I command thee, pick upeth this poppage of corn!"

Nothing happened.

"Why won't this thing work anymore?" she fumed.

She dumped another scoopful of popcorn on the floor.

"You know, we were hoping to eat some of that," said one of the moviegoers.

"Mirror, make these annoying people go away," Juniper announced.

They walked away. But Juniper couldn't tell if it was magic or if they were just weirded out. "That kinda worked...." She shrugged.

More and more people were headed into the theater, chattering and excited. Juniper, grumbling, had to serve up popcorn and soda. All she wanted was to sneak another look at her mirror.

"Juniper Montage!" called out a surprised voice.

Juniper cringed instinctively. She wanted to hide. She didn't want anyone who knew her to see what her new job was.

Of course, it was the girls from Canterlot High. They'd all agreed to meet at the mall to go to the movies. They were just waiting for Sunset Shimmer and Starlight Glimmer to arrive. But the last person in the world they had expected to run into was Juniper Montage.

"What in the blazes are you doing here?" asked Applejack.

"Were you invited to the *Daring Do* premiere?" Pinkie Pie couldn't believe it, especially after everything that had happened. "That's exciting. No, crazy. No, concerning. No! Just… *no!*"

Pinkie Pie blushed, embarrassed by her own outburst. "No offense," she apologized.

"I wasn't invited to the premiere," explained Juniper Montage. "My uncle, Canter Zoom, felt bad for firing me, so he pulled some strings and got me this job."

Fluttershy gulped, strangely unnerved. "You work here?"

"As little as possible," answered Juniper, raising an eyebrow. Oh, she wanted to look at herself saying that. She imagined that the mirror would show her how haughty and powerful she looked.

"You know," said Rainbow Dash, "if you hadn't tried to sabotage the movie, you could be celebrating with us."

Juniper's eyes lit up with rage. "This should be *my* night! I would have found a way to be in the film if you all had stayed out of it. I would have been famous! Everyone would have loved me! *See?*"

Juniper held up the mirror so everyone could see how glamorous and popular she was. But all the other girls saw were their own everyday reflections.

"What is she talking about?" wondered Twilight Sparkle in a low voice to the others.

"Not a clue!"

"What is with her?"

"Two apples short of a bushel, I say," whispered Applejack.

Juniper stamped her foot. "Can't you see what's right under your noses? *Ugh! I wish you'd all go away and leave me alone!*"

The mirror flashed. It shimmered. It sparkled. It trembled.

"What's happening?" wondered Twilight Sparkle, sensing mischievous magic on the loose.

Juniper's eyes widened. "I'm not sure." But she had a terrible, awful, horrible feeling that the girls were about to disappear like kernels of popcorn.

Womp! Twilight Sparkle was gone!

"It ate her!" screeched Pinkie Pie. "Like a hungry monster mirror magnet!"

Womp! Womp! Womp!

One by one, every one of the girls disappeared.

Juniper watched—stunned, amazed, delighted. She saw Fluttershy's barrette on the ground and picked it up. She pinned it triumphantly onto her lapel near her name tag. She was going to win after all. That's what the mirror was telling her!

She spun it around and looked at her face, surrounded by adoring fans. "Hi, me!" Just behind her own smiling visage and the adoring crowds, she saw the girls trapped inside the glass. *"Hmm,"* she mused. "Looks like I may finally be getting the hang of this."

There was no telling what she could do now!

CHAPTER

17

Worries and Concerns

★ ★ ★

Sunset Shimmer looked down at her phone, worried. "Six cell phones, all straight to voice mail," she said anxiously.

She and Starlight Glimmer had arrived at the mall on time, but Sunset Shimmer thought she'd seen a wisp of magic near the sunglasses stand. She and Starlight Glimmer had tried to track it down, but they couldn't find it—and now they couldn't find their friends. Why weren't they answering their phones?

"I'm sure they're around," Starlight Glimmer said reassuringly. "We are only a few minutes late. What's the worst that could have happened?"

Sunset Shimmer was thinking about all the out-of-control magic she'd witnessed since coming to Canterlot High. She sighed. "Our friends are probably fine. I'm overreacting. But maybe not. I can't tell anymore."

"You've wanted to talk to Princess Twilight about this, right? Because you can still talk it over with me if you want."

Sunset Shimmer smiled. She really liked Starlight Glimmer.

"Or you could just journal with Princess Twilight about it. That's a good idea, too," suggested Starlight Glimmer.

"I know my friends and I have been given special powers for a reason," Sunset Shimmer confided. "And I want to be ready for whatever is going to be thrown at us." Sunset Shimmer was wearing her geode necklace again. She touched it protectively. She could tell that something was about to go haywire. Thanks to the necklace, she could feel it. But she didn't know what was about to happen. Still, it made her feel a whole lot better to have a friend from Equestria at her side.

"My advice," offered Starlight Glimmer, "would be to just trust that things will work themselves out in the end. If you spend too much time worrying about the bad things that *might* happen, you'll miss out on all the good things that *are* happening."

Sunset Shimmer blushed. "Like the fact that the pony who was supposed to come here and learn a lesson about friendship is kind of teaching me one right now."

"Yeah." Starlight Glimmer laughed loudly. "Like that."

"Come on," said Sunset Shimmer. "Let's go look around the theater. I'm sure they're fine."

CHAPTER

18

Nowhere and Nothing

✦ ✦ ✦

The girls were lost in a strange limbo between the worlds. All around them was, well, nothing. It was like being in a vast, silent, empty room. But they could see one another—and that was better than nothing.

Pinkie Pie stepped forward, and her

footsteps sent booming echoes through the eerie quiet. It was very strange.

Rarity shivered. "Any clue yet where we are or what just happened? Anyone?"

Pinkie Pie was investigating the perimeters of the space. "Nope, no wall over here. Come out, come out, wherever you are, walls!"

She raced forward until she was far in the distance, a tiny dot. "I don't get this place," she shouted back. "There are no walls in here anywhere."

Applejack was thinking. "Somehow, someway, that dang Juniper sucked us all inside that mirror of hers."

"Or into some lost world behind it," worried Twilight Sparkle.

"I think I might be freaking out a little

bit," murmured Fluttershy, her voice trembling.

"On the upside," said Pinkie Pie, walking back to her friends, "there's popcorn in here!" She munched on a handful she'd found.

Rarity didn't feel relieved. "How could this happen the evening of my first movie premiere? Of all nights! Curse you, oh cruel, cruel fate!"

"Not our number-one problem right now, Rarity," snapped Rainbow Dash.

"Is there really no way outta here?" asked Applejack. They were a good team. They were problem solvers. They could figure this out, right?

Ping! Ping! Ping!

Small brown pellets were launching

through the air, hitting the girls on their heads.

"Ouch! Ouch! Ouch!" they screeched.

"Oh my heavens! What was that?" cried Rarity.

Rainbow Dash was looking at one of them, which she'd caught in her hand. "Chocolate-covered almonds?"

"Dibs!" Pinkie Pie called. They might not be able to figure out where they were or how to escape, but at least the treats were yummy. Pinkie Pie always tried to look on the bright side of things.

CHAPTER

19

Friends and Faults

★ ★ ★

Juniper was holding up the mirror, using it to vacuum up a spilled box of chocolate almonds. When she was done, she admired her reflection. Really, she was getting prettier and more important every time she looked.

Sunset Shimmer spotted her across the

lobby and couldn't believe it. "It's Juniper Montage!" She gasped.

"No!" said Starlight Glimmer instinctively "Who's that?"

"Trouble." Sunset Shimmer nodded grimly. "She's trouble." She was even more worried when she saw that Juniper Montage was wearing a pin that looked an awful lot like Fluttershy's barrette.

"Wait for me here," she instructed Starlight Glimmer. She needed to investigate. Starlight hung back and peeked around the corner to watch what was happening.

Juniper Montage seemed unexpectedly happy to see Sunset Shimmer. "I was wondering when you'd show up," she said, smiling.

"I'm really just looking for my friends,"

Sunset Shimmer told her. "I don't suppose you've seen them?"

Juniper giggled.

"Where are they?!" Sunset Shimmer demanded to know.

"I'll never tell," answered Juniper Montage coyly.

"You don't have to!" With one hand, Sunset Shimmer held her geode, and with the other, she touched Juniper's shoulder. She looked into her eyes—and fell into Juniper's mind. She immediately saw a memory.

Canter Zoom was talking to Juniper Montage in the lobby of the cinema. "You're lucky I offered to get you this job after the stunt you pulled on my set," he was telling her.

"I just wanted to be Daring Do," grumbled Juniper. "I just wanted people to like me."

Now Sunset Shimmer saw Juniper Montage watching the dance video. She could see her thoughts. *Everyone would love me if it weren't for you girls. This is all your fault.*

Poor Juniper Montage, thought Sunset Shimmer. What she really needed wasn't popularity or admiration; what she needed were friends.

But knowing that didn't make her any less dangerous. That's when Sunset Shimmer saw a more recent memory: Juniper wishing that the girls would disappear and sucking them up into her mirror.

Sunset Shimmer backed away quickly from Juniper Montage. She knew she was dangerous, but she hadn't realized she also had magical powers.

Juniper's eyes narrowed. "What? What?"

"I know you want people to like you,"

Sunset Shimmer said carefully. "But trust me, the magic in that mirror is only going to make things worse for you."

Juniper tossed her hair. "You're just saying that because you want the mirror for yourself."

"What I want is my friends back. Please, Juniper. You wished them into that mirror. Maybe there is a way you can wish them out."

"Or maybe," cackled Juniper, "I wish you'd join them!"

Whoosh!

A beam of magic shot out of the mirror like a lasso and wrapped itself around Sunset Shimmer, sucking her into the reflected limbo.

"Sunset!" called Starlight Glimmer.

But it was too late. She was gone.

CHAPTER

20

Stars and Shards

⭐ ⭐ ⭐

Sunset Shimmer flew into the limbo like she'd been shot out of a cannon. She hurtled past the cluster of girls, tumbled over and over, and finally stumbled woozily to her feet.

"Sunset Shimmer!" exclaimed Twilight Sparkle, surprised to see her.

"Hurray!" Pinkie Pie shouted. "We're all together again!"

Fluttershy felt something pulsing at her neck. It was her geode. Its light dimmed and brightened, dimmed and brightened. The geodes all the other girls were wearing flashed, too.

"Um…" noted Fluttershy, barely able to talk.

"But wait," realized Twilight Sparkle, a look of horror on her face. "If we're all together, then nobody out there knows where we are!"

"Starlight Glimmer does!" Sunset Shimmer told them.

"Um…g-girls…" Fluttershy stuttered. But she was speaking too softly for anyone to hear. The geodes were glowing now.

"Whoa!" said Rainbow Dash, suddenly noticing. "Check out our geodes!"

"That's what I was trying to say!" A relieved Fluttershy sighed.

Not only were the geodes pulsing, but the empty space where the girls were seemed to be vibrating to the same rhythm.

"Something's changed," Twilight Sparkle noted. "This wasn't happening before."

"Maybe it's because all seven of us are together now," suggested Sunset Shimmer.

Applejack pursed her lips. "Is that a good thing or a bad thing?"

Beams of energy shot out of their geodes at the exact same moment. They lit up the frame of the mirror that trapped them.

Rarity gasped. "Oh dear. I'm not so sure this is a good thing!"

"Check it out!" exclaimed Rainbow Dash, investigating. She was peering around the mirror frame. Everyone joined her. What could she see?

They could see Juniper Montage's face looking into the mirror.

With each pulse of the mirror in her hand, Juniper was changing. She was growing taller, her hair was curling, her face was sharpening. Her uniform was even becoming an evening gown. She was turning into her enchanted reflection.

"Everyone will finally recognize I'm a star!" Juniper's bright-green eyes glittered. "Now to sign some autographs!"

She stomped past Starlight Glimmer without seeing her. She glided through the mall. She felt perfectly glamorous, but she didn't have any idea how terrifying she was. She was twice as tall as everyone else! People fled as soon as they saw her. They didn't want an autograph; they wanted to get away!

Starlight Glimmer tailed her, trying to figure out what to do. "Okay, first things first. I need to get that magic mirror away from her."

Cowering mall-goers snapped photos of the strange monster stomping past the stores. Juniper thought they were paparazzi and posed, smiling. She saw a small child eating an ice cream cone with his mother and approached them.

"Want Mommy to take our picture together?" she asked, grinning.

The child burst into tears and leaped into his mother's arms.

"Juniper Montage! Juniper Montage!" called Starlight Glimmer. "I'm from the..."

uh...um...*Canterlot Times.* I'm writing an exclusive...."

Juniper spun around. "An exclusive?"

"Yes," said Starlight Glimmer, thinking fast. "About the secret to your amazing success. I'd love to get an interview."

Juniper Montage sighed happily. "But of course!"

"Great! Maybe you could take me somewhere a little quieter so we won't be interrupted by all your adoring fans?"

"Good idea," answered Juniper. "I don't think you'd be able to hear a thing over my screaming fans."

A patron had just seen Juniper and run howling with terror into a department store. Juniper waved before heading back toward the theater lobby.

The moment Juniper wasn't looking,

Starlight Glimmer lunged—and snatched the mirror. Juniper was furious! Both their hands were on the mirror, tugging at it. Starlight Glimmer wouldn't let go. Juniper wouldn't let go. But the mirror flew out of their hands anyway. It dropped on the ground—and cracked.

CHAPTER

21

Mistakes and Forgiveness

★ ★ ★

The girls felt the glass crack. The invisible world around them began to shake. Huge cracks appeared under their feet. The girls screamed.

"The mirror is breaking!" shouted Sunset Shimmer.

"If Starlight Glimmer doesn't find a way

to get us out of here soon, I don't know what's going to happen," Twilight Sparkle cried.

Starlight Glimmer's face appeared in the mirror frame.

"I hope you know what you're doing," whispered Sunset Shimmer.

The girls heard Juniper Montage screaming, "Give that back!"

"No," Starlight Glimmer refused. "This mirror is nothing but trouble. You have to realize that."

"What I realize," said Juniper Montage, "is that you are just like those other girls. I wish you'd join them."

Starlight Glimmer braced herself, preparing to disappear. But nothing happened. "Looks like you can't make that wish unless you're the one holding the mirror," she realized. "I wish Sunset Shimmer and her friends would come back."

But nothing happened.

Juniper smiled. "Looks like you can't use it, either! Might as well give it back to me."

Juniper lunged toward the mirror, but Starlight Glimmer jumped away from her. A shard from the broken mirror splintered and fell out.

Fluttershy screamed as she teetered toward a gaping hole of nothingness inside the mirror. Sunset Shimmer grabbed ahold of her, and Rainbow Dash grabbed Sunset Shimmer. But there was nothing else in their strange limbo world to hold on to but one another.

Juniper Montage could not take her eyes off the mirror in Starlight Glimmer's hands.

"I'll return the mirror," Starlight Glimmer

told her. "But if its magic still works for you, you have to try and use it to bring the girls back."

"And why in the world should I do that?"

Starlight Glimmer took a deep breath. She thought about everything she'd learned about friendship—in Equestria and since coming to Canterlot High. "I overheard Sunset saying that you want to be liked. I have to believe that deep down you know this isn't the way to make that happen."

"Isn't it?" sneered Juniper Montage. "Those girls took away any other chance I had of being famous."

She lunged again toward Starlight. Starlight lifted the mirror over her head— and another shard crashed to the ground.

The girls inside the mirror screamed. What would happen if they went from limbo into nothingness? Where would they be then?

But Rarity remembered her geode! She clutched it. She activated it—and a diamond dome shielded the girls from the gaping abyss. But how long would it last? What if more cracks, and more unfathomable crevices, appeared?

Starlight knew the girls were in danger. She had to act fast. "Is fame really what you're after?" she asked Juniper Montage. "Or are you looking for something else?"

Juniper's brow furrowed. "Like what?"

"Like," said Starlight softly, "a friend."

Juniper sniffed. "Who would want to be my friend? If I'm famous, people have to like me."

"I want to be your friend." Starlight Glimmer reached out her hand.

But Juniper Montage didn't trust her. "Why?"

"Because I understand you, Juniper. You're angry, hurt, and sad. You think getting revenge is going to make you feel better, but it's not! Please don't make a mistake that you'll end up regretting for the rest of your life."

Juniper Montage hung her head in shame. "I've already made too many mistakes. What I've done is…unforgivable."

"No, Juniper," said Starlight Glimmer, trying to reassure her. "I have a feeling they'll forgive you. But first, you have to set them free!"

She knew she was taking a big risk, but Starlight Glimmer held out the mirror to Juniper Montage.

There were gaping cracks everywhere

inside the mirror. The girls were slipping and sliding toward them. The dome couldn't protect them from the void much longer.

Juniper greedily grabbed the mirror. She gazed at its surface. But this time she did not see herself. She saw the girls, afraid and in danger.

"I wish I could make up for my mistakes," murmured Juniper.

More cracks cut through the white expanse of nothingness. The dome disappeared. The girls were all careering in different directions. All hope seemed lost.

Boom!

The girls burst out of the mirror into the lobby of the movie theater.

"Starlight, you did it!" exclaimed Sunset Shimmer with relieved gratitude.

A crowd of people was clustering around, trying to figure out what was happening.

"So much for laying low." Starlight Glimmer shrugged.

"I think even Princess Twilight would understand," Sunset Shimmer reassured her.

Juniper was back to her normal self. When she looked in what was left of the mirror, all she could see was her plain, regular, ordinary face.

She put down the mirror. "I'm so sorry," she said. But unlike when she had apologized for disrupting the Daring Do movie, this time she meant it.

The girls recognized her sincerity.

"It's okay," said Sunset Shimmer kindly. "We've all been there."

"Really?" Juniper Montage didn't believe that.

Starlight Glimmer raised her hand. "I manipulated an entire town into giving up their talents so they wouldn't think they were special."

Twilight Sparkle stepped forward. "Overpowered by a magic I couldn't control and created a rift between two worlds, almost destroying both of them in the process."

"Turned the whole school into my own personal zombie army at Fall Formal," Sunset Shimmer admitted.

Juniper's mouth hung open.

"Wow!" said Pinkie Pie. "We *are* a really forgiving group."

Everyone burst out laughing. It was true. They were.

Juniper Montage pointed up at the video screen. "You are also an award-winning group," she said.

"What?" exclaimed Sunset Shimmer. Could it be true?

"What are you talking about?" Rarity held her breath. If they had won, they would get the prize money and be able to pay for the repairs Camp Everfree needed. Her plan would have worked!

"Is that our video?" whispered Flutter-shy, amazed.

"It is! It is! It is!" Pinkie Pie was jump-ing up and down. "We won the dance video contest!"

"And the prize money!" shouted Rain-bow Dash, pumping her fist in the air.

"Dance Magic" was the winning video. The girls had done it.

They had saved Camp Everfree again.

Not only that, they had saved Juniper

Montage from herself. And they had made a wonderful new friend in Starlight Glimmer. Once again, they had shown that the best magic was always the Magic of Friendship. With friendship, you could do anything.

CHAPTER

22

Endings and...
Beginnings!

★ ★ ★

It was time for Starlight Glimmer to head back to Equestria. The girls clustered around the statue of the Wondercolt.

"I'm so sad to leave," said Starlight Glimmer. "I haven't really had the chance to get to know all of you!"

Sunset Shimmer was just about to say

something when her journal began to glow. A message was appearing. She quickly opened it up to find out what Princess Twilight had to say. She smiled as she read. "Maybe you don't have to leave yet!"

The girls cheered.

Sunset Shimmer read out loud the message from Equestria. *"Dear Sunset Shimmer. Some lessons are better learned in action, and you girls are great teachers. Starlight should stay for a few more days. At least until you find out how the Daring Do movie is doing!"*

Starlight Glimmer beamed with happiness. "I think she means you, too, Sunset. Think you can focus on the positive and not worry too much about out-of-control magic?"

"Whatever happens is going to happen," realized Sunset Shimmer. "Not much I can do about it, so I've just gotta live in the moment, right?"

"Right!" agreed Starlight Glimmer.

Magical things were always going to happen, but if you had friends, nothing would ever go wrong for very long.

HooRay foR appLewood!

The girls get to visit the set of the
Daring Do movie, and then they get to
attend its premiere! What will they wear?
How will they do their hair? Each girl has
her own special style, but that doesn't mean
she doesn't need a little help getting her
fashions ready for these A-list events. Can
you help each girl get ready for the red
carpet? What special skills and talents do *you*
have to be a stylist to the stars?

_____

_____

_____

_____

_____

_____

_____

_____

SUNSET SHIMMER'S SASSY STYLE

Sunset Shimmer is a natural leader with an edgy taste when it comes to her clothes. She bought a new jacket for opening night. Give it a special color that she is sure to love!

APPLEJACK FORGOT HER SHOES!

Oh no! Applejack, the country girl
with homespun style, forgot to pack her
footwear for the big event. Which pair
would you get for her at the store? Circle
the ones that she is sure to love!

PiNKie PiE'S PaLS!

Pinkie Pie is looking for some inspiration! She loves everything pink, of course, and that includes pink flowers, pink sequins, pink balloons, and pink prints of all kinds. Which celebrities have a style just like hers? Who would you tell her to look at for some fashion dos?

1 _____

2 _____

3 _____

4 _____

5 _____

6 _____

7 _____

RaRity's one of a KinD

When it comes to fashion, Rarity leads the way! She never looks just like anyone else—but she always looks just right. Can you spot the stand-out Rarity, the one that's just a little bit different, and absolutely perfect?

FLUTTERSHY'S FLOWER POWER!

Fluttershy's look is soft, flowing, and
flowery! Forget the sparkling jewels and
the glittering bling! Help Fluttershy
decorate her dress and her hair with
the prettiest flowers ever!

RAINBOW DASH IS In It to *Win It!*

So little time and so much to pack!
What must-have accessories should
Rainbow Dash put in her suitcase?
Shoot her a quick text and tell this
sporty athlete which three to include:

1 _____

2 _____

3 _____

NeW GiRL in TOWn!

Starlight Glimmer has just arrived at Canterlot High…and the world of human beings! She's going to need some tips as she puts together her school-day outfits. Can you offer her some Fashion Dos…and some Fashion Don'ts?

FASHION DOS

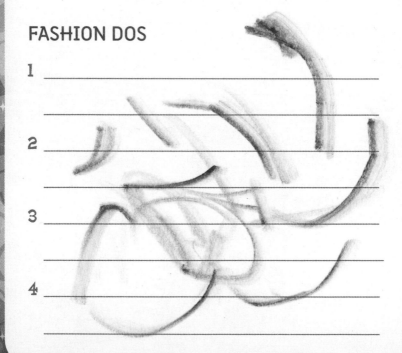

1 _____

2 _____

3 _____

4 _____

FASHION DON'TS

1 _____

_____

2 _____

_____

3 _____

_____

4 _____

_____

HiGHLiGHtiNG TWiLiGHt SPARKLe

Wherever she goes, Twilight Sparkle stands
out from the crowd! She's getting her hair
done especially for the premiere.
Can you help her make it shine?
What colors should it be?

MiRROR, MiRROR on tHe WaLL!

When you look in the mirror, what do you see? Which Equestria Girl shares your hobbies, your interests, and your sense of style? Which girl is most like *you*?

BOOK CLUB!

Everyone knows that Rainbow Dash is a fan of Daring Do, but what do you think are the other girls' favorite books? If you had to guess, which book would you put at their top of their list?

Rainbow Dash _____ Daring Do _____

Fluttershy _____

Rarity _____

Sunset Shimmer _____

Applejack _____

Twilight Sparkle _____

Pinkie Pie _____

GEODE SUPERPOWERS

At Camp Everfree, each girl discovered
that she had a special superpower.
Match the girl with her power!

Rarity   exploding sparkles

Fluttershy   diamond force fields

Sunset Shimmer   super speed

Twilight Sparkle   mind reading

Rainbow Dash   talking to animals

Applejack   magic

Pinkie Pie   strength

WHaT IS *YOUR* SUPERPOWER?

Imagine you visited the Crystal Cave at Camp
Everfree and got your own geode. What special
abilities or talents of yours would it enhance?
How would it let you help other people the way
the Equestria Girls help their friends?
Write your own geode adventure!